AF751707

First published 2022 by
FREMANTLE PRESS

This edition first published 2024.

Fremantle Press Inc. trading as Fremantle Press
PO Box 158, North Fremantle, Western Australia, 6159
fremantlepress.com.au

Copyright text © Dianne Wolfer, 2022
Copyright illustrations © Brian Simmonds, 2022

The moral rights of the creators have been asserted.

This book is copyright. Apart from any fair dealing for the purpose of private study, research, criticism or review, as permitted under the *Copyright Act*, no part may be reproduced by any process without written permission. Every reasonable effort has been made to seek permission for quotations contained herein. Please address any enquiries to the publisher.

Cover and digital collages designed by Rebecca Mills, rebeccamills.com.au
Printed by Leo Paper Products Ltd. Guangdong, China

A catalogue record for this book is available from
the National Library of Australia.

ISBN 9781760994372 (hardback)

Fremantle Press is supported by the State Government through the Department of Local Government, Sport and Cultural Industries.

Fremantle Press respectfully acknowledges the Whadjuk people of the Noongar nation as the Traditional Owners and Custodians of the land where we work in Walyalup.

The Last Light Horse

Dianne Wolfer

illustrated by Brian Simmonds

FREMANTLE PRESS

down through the last glimmer of twilight, stepping high and free,
like a cloud, a moth, a ghost in the shape of a horse

—Elyne Mitchell

PART I

Francis

The newborn foal tested his hooves.

Frost crackled as his legs slipped further apart.

Mother nudged him to try again.

Sandy was soon frisking with the other foals. They shivered when the wild brumbies whinnied on winter evenings and chased Bogong moths in the spring. Sandy grew bold in the crisp mountain air.

Summer came and eucalypts burst into flower. The horses lazed in their lush paddock swishing blowflies with their tails. As the moths flew back from their summer migration the nights became cooler. Once again frost crackled under Sandy's hooves.

Sandy's bay coat darkened and he grew to over 15 hands high. During his third winter, Sandy wore a bridle and saddle. He learned to carry a rider on his back. That felt strange at first. Sandy was skittish, but roaming beyond the home paddock was exciting. There was so much to discover.

One morning a stranger opened the gate.

'G'day,' he called. 'You must be Sandy, I'm Francis.'

The man held something sweet-smelling. Sandy nibbled. The apple was like sunshine on crunchy snow.

Francis took Sandy to work at his family kiln in Tallangatta. Carting bricks was heavy work but Francis was patient. He taught Sandy to stand steady while loading and to brace his legs on steep hills.

'Well done,' Francis said as he unbuckled Sandy's harness each afternoon and gave him an apple or a carrot.

After chomping his treat, Sandy trotted into a meadow with other horses. He shook his mane and rolled onto his back, scratching the day away.

Francis rode Sandy to football games in winter and they cantered through the high country in summer, following wild brumbies and startling wombats.

In August 1914, Francis returned from town, waving a newspaper.

'War's been declared,' he shouted. 'I'm going to join up.'

'Our bishop will have something to say about that,' Francis' brother muttered. 'He'll not be letting an Irishman join a British battalion.'

'But I'm Australian.'

'Tis the same army,' his brother replied.

A notice went around the district.

The government needed to buy horses for the war. There was going to be a muster at Tallangatta. Francis cantered Sandy to the saleyards to watch the excitement.

Declaration of War!

Excitement was keen on Wednesday with news that war has broken out between Great Britain and Germany. Following this announcement, Prime Minister Cook confirmed that Australia is also at war.

The Governor-General has received a cable expressing His Majesty the King's appreciation of Australia's offer of an expeditionary force.

Men, nurses and horses will be sent to the aid of the Motherland.

HORSES NEEDED FOR THE EXPEDITIONARY FORCES

The Minister of Defence is looking to purchase horses for the use of the Australian Expeditionary Forces. Horses are to be 15-16 hands in height and aged between 4-10 years. Greys, washy chestnuts or piebalds will not be accepted. Owners are invited to bring their horses for selection to Tallangatta on 19th August at 9 a.m.

A tall, thin man with bristling energy was also watching the muster. Soldiers and officials stood straight to salute him.

Sandy snorted when the man stopped in front of him.

Major General Bridges laughed.

'What a fine horse,' he told Francis.

'He is that,' Francis replied. 'Nothing special to look at, but raised in the high country, perhaps with a dash of brumby blood.'

'They breed exceptional horses up there. Is he part of the sale?'

'No, Sir, his trade is hauling bricks.'

'Ah, that's a pity. I'm looking for a strong charger.'

Francis stroked Sandy's neck. 'Take him for a ride if you like.'

Instead of signing up, Francis donated the best horse he'd ever known to Major General Bridges and the war effort. As soldiers led away his gentle bay gelding, Francis swallowed his sadness and whispered, 'Do us proud, Sandy.'

At Maribyrnong Remount Depot, Sandy was branded with a government imprint. Then he joined a yard with other sturdy Australian horses known as Walers.

The horses ate chaff from nose bags, while kit weighing 130 kilograms was loaded onto their backs. Sandy stood steady. He was used to hauling heavy loads.

There were new skills to learn: marching, turning back and forth, while the men shouted.

'Sections right.'

'Form troop.'

'Walk, march, halt.'

When the Light Horse soldiers yelled, 'Charge', the horses galloped. Sandy had a broad back and his gait was sure, but some riders still fell off. No soldier was as kind as Francis, and no one brought him apples.

'Hello again,' Major General Bridges said when he saw Sandy. 'How's your training going?'

They walked around the yard, then cantered beside the river. After trotting back, the major general stroked the white blaze on Sandy's forehead and said, 'I think you'll do nicely.'

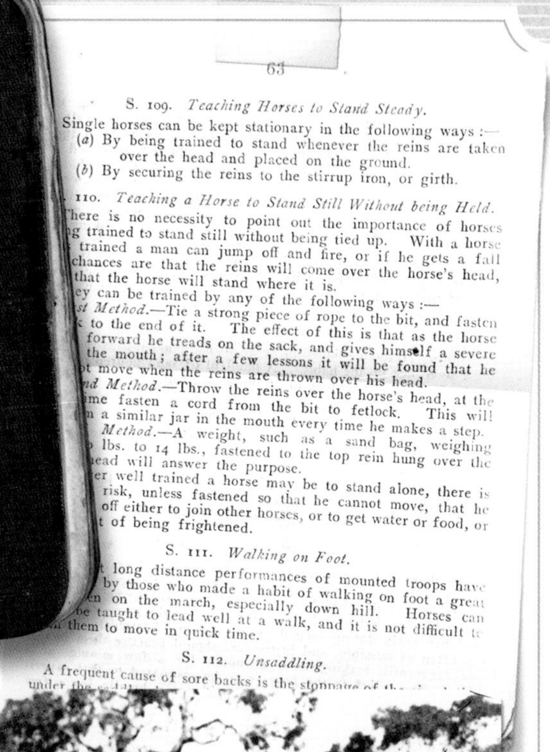

63

S. 109. *Teaching Horses to Stand Steady.*

Single horses can be kept stationary in the following ways :—
(*a*) By being trained to stand whenever the reins are taken over the head and placed on the ground.
(*b*) By securing the reins to the stirrup iron, or girth.

110. *Teaching a Horse to Stand Still Without being Held.*

There is no necessity to point out the importance of horses g trained to stand still without being tied up. With a horse trained a man can jump off and fire, or if he gets a fall chances are that the reins will come over the horse's head, that the horse will stand where it is.

ey can be trained by any of the following ways :—

st *Method.*—Tie a strong piece of rope to the bit, and fasten to the end of it. The effect of this is that as the horse forward he treads on the sack, and gives himself a severe the mouth; after a few lessons it will be found that he ot move when the reins are thrown over his head.

nd *Method.*—Throw the reins over the horse's head, at the me fasten a cord from the bit to fetlock. This will a similar jar in the mouth every time he makes a step.

Method.—A weight, such as a sand bag, weighing lbs. to 14 lbs., fastened to the top rein hung over the ead will answer the purpose.

er well trained a horse may be to stand alone, there is risk, unless fastened so that he cannot move, that he off either to join other horses, or to get water or food, or t of being frightened.

S. 111. *Walking on Foot.*

t long distance performances of mounted troops have by those who made a habit of walking on foot a great en on the march, especially down hill. Horses can be taught to lead well at a walk, and it is not difficult to them to move in quick time.

S. 112. *Unsaddling.*

A frequent cause of sore backs is the stoppage of the ...

I can make a General in
five minutes but a good
horse is hard to replace.
—Abraham Lincoln

PART II

Major General Bridges

Horses jostled and bucked as soldiers pushed them up the gangplank onto the *Orvieto*, flagship of the Australian fleet.

They set sail mid-afternoon on 21 October 1914. A band on the wharf played *God Save the King* followed by a rousing rendition of *Rule Britannia*.

Three of the horses on board *Orvieto* belonged to Major General Bridges: Sandy, Pascha and Brown Mare.

Pascha was the beauty. He was dark and glossy with a proud bearing. Sandy was even-tempered and Brown Mare was steady; not even the foghorn spooked her.

Accompanying the horses were 1,453 men and four nurses.

2. *Transport by Sea.*—Detailed instructions as regards the embarkation, disembarkation, and the duties on board ship should be carefully studied by the staff and squadron officers.

Standing orders—printed, if possible—should be drawn up beforehand and published, so that all ranks may thoroughly understand the routine of embarkation and the duties on board ship.

S. 357. CROSSING RIVERS.

1. *Fording.*—The selection of a ford and the crossing of rivers with mounted troops are operations requiring experience and care.

If the fords are deep and dangerous, the bits should be removed from the horses' mouths, and the men warned to disengage their feet from their stirrups, being at the same time reminded of the principles necessary if required to swim. It may sometimes be advisable to station a few expert swimmers and a rope at or below the ford.

The following depths are fordable :—

For infantry, 3 feet.
For cavalry, 4 feet.
Waggons containing ammunition, 2 feet 4 inches.

Gravelly bottoms are best, sandy bottoms are bad, as the sand gets stirred up, and increases the depth.

The depth of a river is generally most uniform in straight parts; at bends the depth will generally be greater at the concave bank, and less at the convex.

For this reason a river which is not anywhere fordable straight across may be found passable in a slanting direction between two bends.

A raft capable of carrying 13 horses can be constructed of four piers, each consisting of seven (100-gallon) casks, bearing a platform 20 feet long and 10 feet wide, provided with a rail

Maj.-Gen. Sir W. T. BRIDGES

65

S. 116. STABLE DUTIES.

1. The establishment and maintenance of a proper system of stable discipline are of the first importance. Upon this the health and condition of the horses, and consequently the efficiency of the corps, depend. Stable duties must never, therefore, be allowed to sink to the level of a mere fatigue, the same punctuality and regularity is to be observed as for any other parade.

On service in the field and in camp officers attend all stables.

2. On *Stables* sounding the men "*Fall in*" by troops in stable dress with grooming kit, and answer their names

The troop leaders will then detail sufficient men to lead the horses to water, two men to draw the feed, and the remainder to muck out and clean the troop lines while the horses are watering, this work to be completed by the time the horses return. On return of the horses from water each man will take over his horse, secure it on the lines, and commence grooming.

During stable hours no man is to leave the stables or horse lines without the permission of his troop officer, nor is any man to stop grooming to clean his saddlery until his horse is passed as clean. Officers are to watch the men grooming, see that they handle their brushes and curry-combs properly, and that time is not wasted.

Officers will carefully note the condition of a horse's coat, both as to cleanliness and health. The mane and tail should also be examined.

The following routine of stable duties will be adhered to :—

Commence grooming the horse at the neck on the near side, work round to the neck on the off side, the legs below the knees and hocks to be left until the body is finished, then thoroughly groom the legs, and pick out feet, sponge eyes, nostrils, and dock, and finish with head; manes and tails to be brushed.

Clean saddlery.

3. Horses are to be led quietly to and from water without trotting or hurrying, and should, when possible, be watered before, and not under ordinary circumstances until two hours after feeding.

C.12294. C

As they sailed west, the men trained for battle, did calisthenics to keep fit and lined up to receive vaccinations against infectious diseases. In the evenings they lazed about, playing games and listening to music.

The seasick horses stayed mostly below deck, struggling to keep their balance. Sandy's stall was squeezed between Brown Mare and Pascha. While Brown Mare endured the voyage quietly, Pascha was edgy. Sandy nuzzled him but the gelding kicked in frustration.

A soldier called Jim filled Sandy's feed bag and checked his hooves. Twice a day he shovelled manure into a bucket attached to a rope.

'Haul away,' Jim yelled to his friend on the top deck each time the bucket was full.

One morning, they anchored in a huge harbour alongside other troopships. Sandy stamped, keen to feel land beneath his hooves.

'There now,' Jim whispered, 'settle down big fella. We've reached Albany's King George Sound, but the likes of us won't be going ashore.'

As Jim led Sandy around the deck, they gazed across the water towards a hill overlooking the harbour. Sandy smelt wildflowers and flared his nostrils.

With the German raider *Emden* prowling the Indian Ocean it was safer for the Australian and New Zealand transports to travel in convoy.

As they left King George Sound, Jim shouted, 'Coo-ee' to a girl on one of the islands. She was standing by a lighthouse waving with all her might.

'What a sight,' he sighed, wiping soot from his eyes as smoke poured from the funnels of thirty-six troopships and their battleship escorts.

The Japanese *Ibuki* and two more troop carriers joined the convoy off the coast of Fremantle. Then they steamed across the Indian Ocean, heading to the battlefields of the First World War.

For Sandy, the days at sea were similar.

Each morning soldiers cleaned the horse stalls and fed the Walers. Matting was laid so the horses could walk on the upper deck.

Grooms rubbed their coats, massaged their swollen legs, then fed them again.

Thirteen days after leaving Albany they reached the Equator. A bugle tooted and soldiers called, 'Make way for King Neptune!'

Sandy watched as a man covered in seaweed strutted across the deck. 'Welcome to the Northern Hemisphere,' King Neptune called.

He poured sweet-smelling treacle over the soldiers then threw them into a large bath. Sandy swished his tail. That bath looked nice and cool ...

'Let's hope the temperature drops now that we've crossed the line,' Jim muttered.

But the humidity continued. Brown Mare chewed her wooden stall. Pascha kicked, and Sandy pawed the deck, longing for frosty grass beneath his hooves.

The convoy reached Colombo and Sandy's nostrils quivered as Jim walked him around the deck.

'Look at those beautiful buildings,' Jim sighed, 'and the palm trees and boats. What a place!'

They sailed on, stopping at Aden, where traders brought strange fruit to barter. Sandy's ears flattened as their shouts filled the air.

Charles Bean

One of Sandy's regular visitors was Charles Bean, Australia's official war correspondent. He was a slim, serious fellow.

'Never mind me,' the war correspondent told the grooms as he sat by the horse stalls adjusting his wire spectacles. 'I'll keep out of your way. I just need a quiet corner to write my notes.'

Major General Bridges also visited. He was aloof with the grooms, but whispered kind words to the Walers as he rubbed their ears.

Finally, in late November, after five weeks at sea, the convoy reached the Suez Canal. The restless horses tossed their heads as they disembarked at Alexandria.

The air was hot and dry and the dock felt like it was swaying. Sandy wobbled like a newborn foal.

After so long at sea, Pascha was also struggling to stand. He bared his teeth as Sandy bumped against him.

Soldiers led the Walers onto a train and they rattled on to Cairo. From there they marched into the desert towards towering pyramids. The exhausted soldiers set up horse-lines in the middle of the night, then fell asleep on the sand. Huge pyramids loomed over their camp.

As their fitness returned, Sandy, Pascha and Brown Mare joined other Walers for long runs into the Egyptian desert. They leapt trenches and practised charging. It was heavy going in the soft sand. Sandy's legs ached at the end of each day.

Major General Bridges was fond of all his horses, but Sandy was his favourite.

'You're no beauty,' he murmured when they rode out to inspect troop-lines or galloped to the pyramids, 'but you understand what I need before I do.'

Although Major General Bridges barked orders to the men, he spoke quietly to Sandy, sometimes about the high country.

'I remember following wild brumbies up near Kosciuszko,' he said, 'on a horse not unlike you. My word, I'd prefer those stately snow gums to this blasted sand.'

January 1915 was cold, with eerie fog and dust storms. Sandy carried Bridges on long troop marches and spent hours watching soldiers pretend to attack each other. When they slept under stars in the desert, beautiful moths twirled around the men's lanterns.

'The ancient Egyptians believed moths were a symbol of the soul,' Bean said one night.

There was a surprised silence. One officer raised an eyebrow and muttered, 'Fascinating!'

Charles Bean smiled and turned back to his notes.

One day Sandy and the major general met Bean riding across the sand on a strange animal.

'Nice day for a camel ride,' Bridges called.

'I've just scrambled to the top of Cheops Pyramid,' the war correspondent replied. 'The view was astounding.'

'Good show, I love climbing the hill to the pyramids at sunset. The sight of 3,000 Australian tents stretched across the sand is a wonder to behold.'

Sandy pawed the sand as the bad-smelling animal stepped closer.

'It's alright, Sandy,' Major General Bridges laughed. 'It's only a camel.'

The animals glared at each other.

Whenever *khamsin* winds blew across the desert, the Walers lowered their heads, huddling together while sand swirled into their eyes, ears and nostrils.

Sandy hated the hot, gritty sand but he stood patiently as bayonets clinked and men shouted.

One morning, Major General Bridges told Sandy, 'There's a big push planned, old fella, and we're going back to sea. You won't like what's ahead.'

He was right.

On 10 April they sailed from Egypt to Lemnos. Sandy and over 6,000 other horses rested on the windswept island for two weeks. Then they reboarded the troopships and sailed towards the Gallipoli Peninsula.

Major General Bridges pressed his face against Sandy's whiskery muzzle.

'I hope we'll meet again,' he whispered as they sailed towards the Gallipoli Peninsula.

In the dark early hours of 25 April explosions filled the air. Horses screamed in terror as the ship's guns boomed. Sandy smelt the sailors' fear and the stink of cordite. He reared, straining to break free as grooms ran in.

'Hey, there, settle!'

'Woah, easy now ...'

A farrier struggled to keep Sandy and the other horses under control while the dreadful shelling boomed on and on.

While Sandy kicked and bucked, the Anzacs were battling to land. Those soldiers who did make it ashore, scrambled for shelter then dug in.

Major General Bridges strode between his scattered units, taking dreadful risks as he tried to inspire confidence in the men.

'Get down, Sir, get down,' a lieutenant shouted on the morning of 14 May. The major general looked around but it was too late. A sniper's bullet had found its mark. Bridges fell, his femoral artery severed.

Stretcher bearers carried him to the beach.

'Don't risk your lives for me,' Bridges implored.

He was evacuated onto a hospital ship but medics could not save the major general and he died a few days later. His last wish was for his favourite horse, Sandy, to be repatriated home to Australia.

Major General Bridges was buried with full military honours in Alexandria. Sandy followed the procession, restless but standing steady.

Reversed boots had been attached to the stirrups of his saddle. They smelt familiar, but there was no major general with the boots.

As the coffin was lowered into the ground *The Last Post* rang out. Sandy tossed his mane, stamping the hot sand and longing for lush, green paddocks.

After resolute persuasion from Bridges' widow, the major general's body was exhumed in July 1915, and returned to Australia. He was buried on a hill in Canberra behind the military college he'd founded.

MAJOR GENERAL BRIDGES KILLED IN COMBAT

The Late Major-General Sir William Throsby BRIDGES, K.C.B., Commander-In-Chief of the Australian Forces, who was wounded in the fighting at the Dardanelles and died at sea while being conveyed to the hospital at Alexandria. He was buried at that city, the funeral being quiet and impressive. General Maxwell, commanding the British forces in Egypt, was present at the graveside. The following message was sent to the Prime Minister by General Sir Ian Hamilton: "General Bridges died on the passage to Alexandria. The whole force mourns a loss of 7000 on the enemy, at a cost of less than 500 to themselves. The news of the distinguished officer's death caused deep regret throughout Australia, for General Bridges was recognised as a brave leader and a brainy organiser and administrator. His work in connection with the Military College at Duntroon will serve as an imperishable monument to his zeal and energy." After vacating the position of Commandant of the Royal Military College, he became Inspector-General of the Commonwealth Forces. He had seen previous active service in the South African campaign, and all who worked under him agree that he was "every inch a soldier". The posthumous honour of Knighthood (K.C.B.) was conferred by the King in recognition of General Bridges' distinguished services.

THE LATE GENERAL BRIDGES : FUNERAL AT CANBERRA

THE body of General Sir William Throsby Bridges, Australia's foremost soldier, who fell at the Dardanelles, was brought to Australia for interment within the grounds of the Duntroon Military College after a concerted campaign by his widow, Lady Bridges. The ceremony took place on Friday last in the presence of the Governor-General and Lady Ferguson, the Prime Minister, the Minister for Defence, the Archbishop of Sydney (who delivered an eloquent panegyric at the graveside), and many others prominent in naval, military, church, political, and civil life.

A horse gallops with his lungs,
Perseveres with his heart,
And wins with his character.
—Federico Tesio

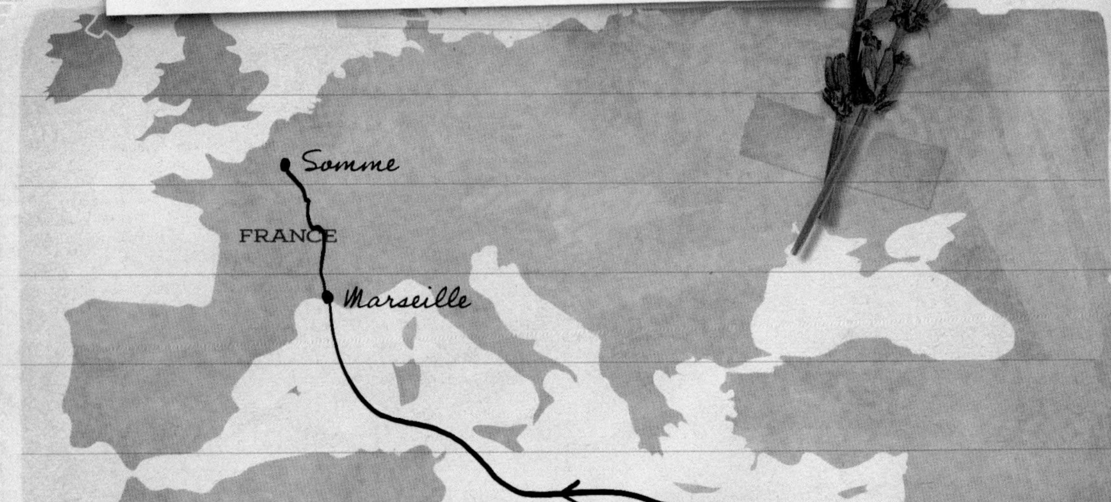

PART III

Whitfield

Sandy stayed in Egypt.

From August 1915, he was under the care of veterinarian, Captain Leslie Whitfield.

'I can see why you were the major general's favourite,' Whitfield laughed as they cantered between desert camps.

The veterinarians treated Walers for mange, exhaustion and equine flu. The worst cases were transported back to the animal hospital for treatment.

Captain Whitfield made sure Sandy was well cared for, just as Francis, Jim and the major general had done before him.

On weekends Sandy joined Pascha and Brown Mare for gallops into the desert. There were dozens of horses, some with riders and some without, kicking their heels into the air for fun.

Sandflies plagued the horses. Sandy flicked his tail and rolled in the sand, trying to ease his itching bites.

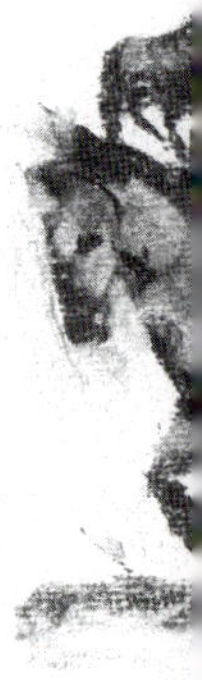

In November the weather turned cold. Whitfield and his team were kept busy treating horses with pneumonia.

January and February 1916 were even more miserable. The horses suffered through winter fog and sandstorms. Despite the hardships, Sandy felt safe with Whitfield. His voice and hands were kind.

'Good news,' Whitfield told Sandy one morning. 'I've received a new posting. I'm off to France and you'll be coming with me.'

In March 1916, Whitfield and Sandy boarded a ship for Marseille. Major General Bridges' horses went their separate ways.

Sandy bucked as a soldier pushed him up the gangway, remembering his last sea voyage. But this journey was shorter. After disembarking they travelled north. Swaying cornflowers and scarlet poppies covered the French fields.

Whitfield and Sandy worked in the area around Bapaume, treating sick donkeys, mules and Walers. Sandy galloped along once-elegant avenues of trees, now blasted to smithereens. Blackened, broken bodies of men and horses lay by the roadsides.

The First Battle of the Somme was a bloodbath. Almost 20,000 British men died on the first day, alongside 6,000 Germans and countless horses from both sides. Sandy and his veterinarian riders cantered to the edges of the battle zones, evacuating injured animals.

Sandy's nostrils flared in the evil smelling air. When he saw Walers wearing strange nose bags, Sandy shied, but before long, he too was wearing a gas mask.

On 23 July the hellish fight for Pozières began. Sandy and the vets evacuated stricken horses. Bean was there too, taking notes and running between trenches, wearing a gas helmet that he complained made it 'impossible to see'.

Winter settled over the shattered land and a third wartime Christmas passed. Whitfield received a Distinguished Service Order in the 1917 Honours List.

'Congratulations, Sir,' the grooms called as the newly promoted 'Major' Whitfield strode past.

Whitfield nodded his thanks and hurried into surgery. There was little time to celebrate.

The January air was bitter and damp, not crisp like a high-country winter. There was no birdsong or sweet eucalyptus breeze. Instead Sandy smelt gunpowder and the stench of death.

Horses arrived suffering terrible wounds and gas burns, and as the heavy shelling continued, Sandy became nervy. Some days he couldn't stop twitching.

'Good news,' Major Whitfield announced one cloudy afternoon. 'We're being transferred again. This time to Calais. I'm going to oversee the building of a new veterinary hospital.'

Sandy lowered his head and whinnied softly as Whitfield stroked his neck.

Major Whitfield's workload increased at Calais, leaving him little time to be with Sandy. When Private Archibald Jordan transferred to the Veterinary Corps, he was appointed as Sandy's groom.

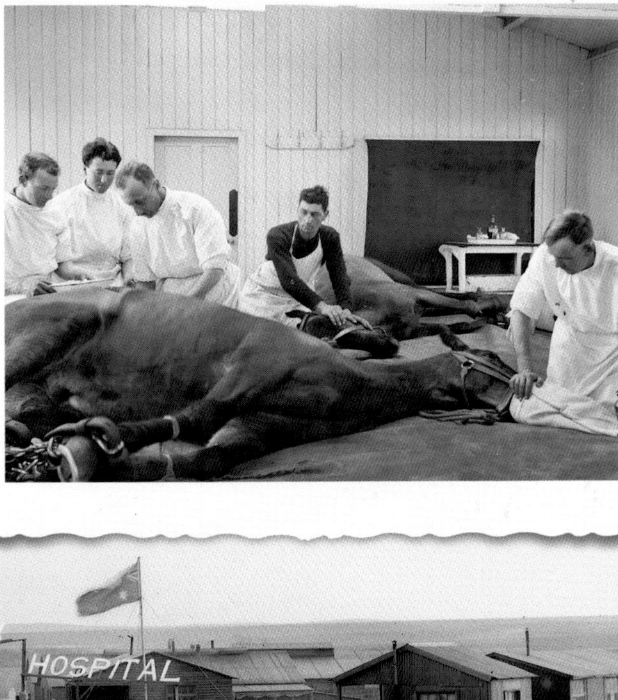

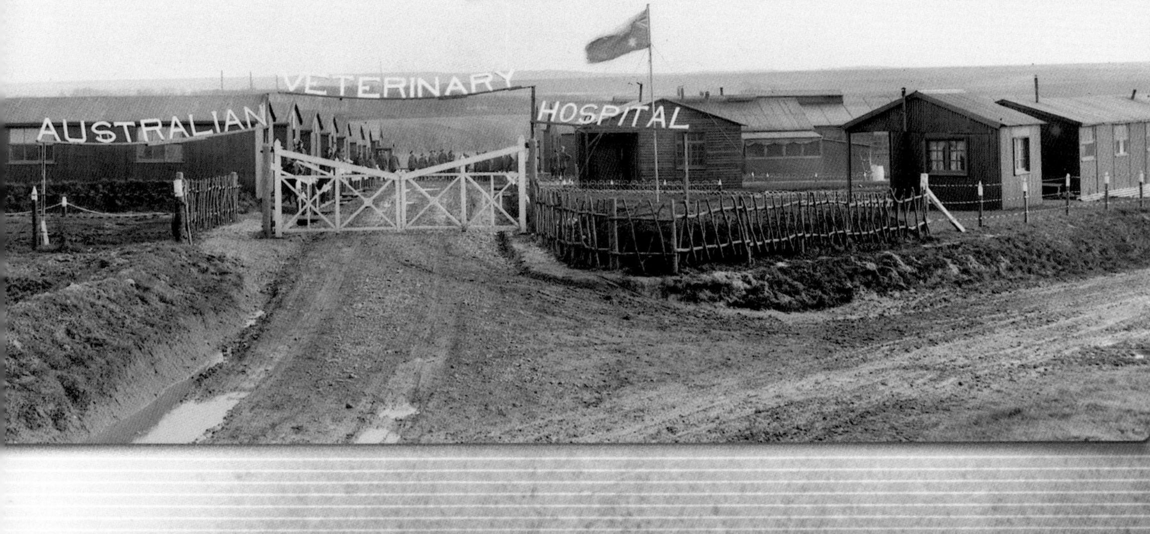
AUSTRALIAN
VETERINARY
HOSPITAL

A horse loves freedom, and the weariest old work horse will roll on the ground or break into a lumbering gallop when he is turned loose into the open.

– Gerald Raftery

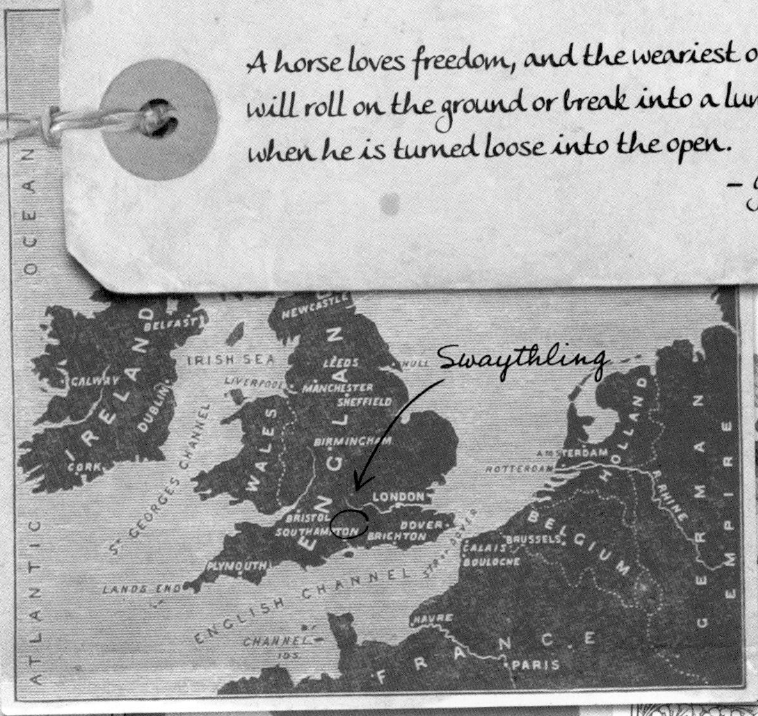

PART IV

Archie

Archie did his best to keep Sandy well. He was a shy fellow who'd fought at Lone Pine, Pozières, the Somme and Mouquet Farm; some of the worst battlefields. Sudden noises startled him.

Whenever Archie was anxious, he hummed, *Keep the Home Fires Burning* and tossed his lucky coin.

'See this shilling,' he told Sandy, 'it's from my sweetheart. I wonder whether she'll be waiting for me at the Melbourne dock when all this is over.'

Sandy nuzzled his gentle groom.

At the end of each day, Archie massaged Sandy and checked his hooves. The roads were littered with nails and shrapnel. If metal flecks were not quickly removed, horses became lame.

The United States entered the war in early April 1917, and American soldiers began arriving in France. Then later that year thousands of men and animals died at Ypres and Passchendaele.

Sandy's nervous twitching worsened. He stopped eating. Archie nestled his face in the Waler's warm neck.

'Hey now mate, you can't just give up,' he coaxed, 'I understand how you feel ...' Archie held softened oats under Sandy's muzzle, 'but I've already lost too many mates. If I lose you, big fella, I don't know how I'd carry on.'

Sandy shuddered and nibbled the mash from Archie's hand.

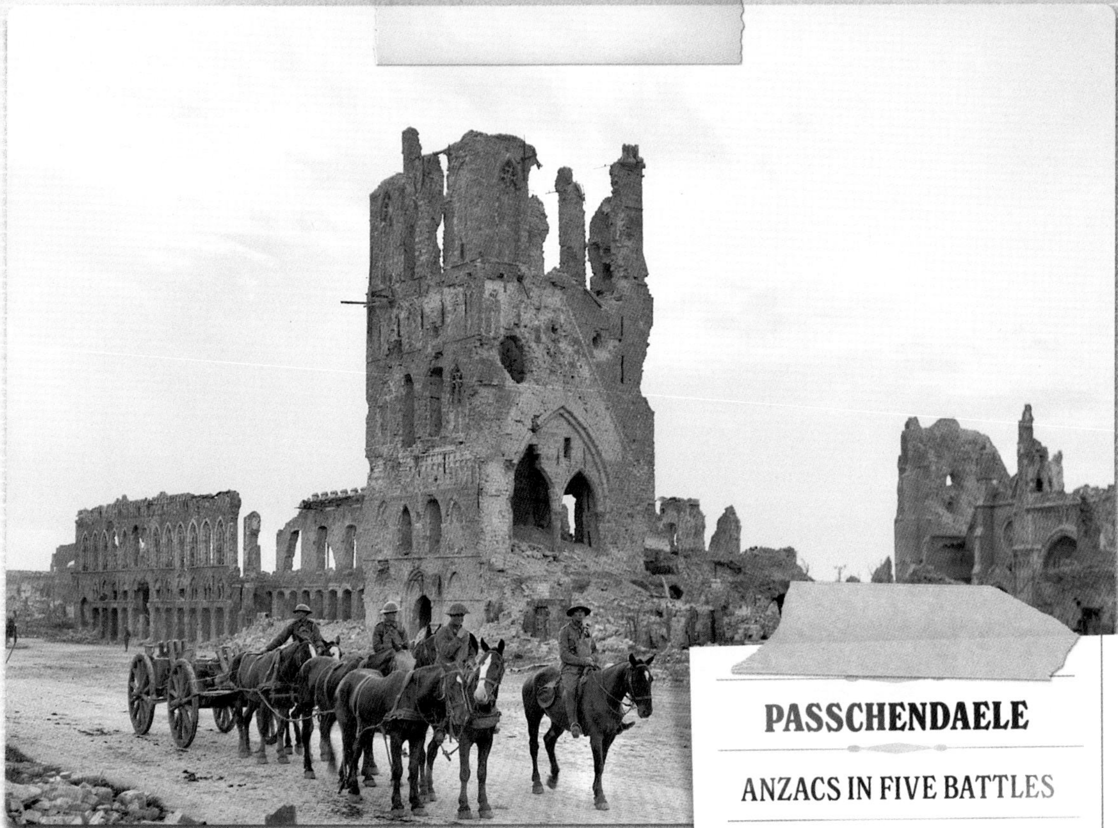

PASSCHENDAELE

ANZACS IN FIVE BATTLES

AT THE FRONT, October: Australia and New Zealand have been fighting for the ridge that is crowned by Passchendaele. The place is no more than a name to many people overseas, but to the soldiers who have fought there this culminating point of the low ridge east of ruined Ypres will ever be a glorious memory.

OUR GREATEST BATTLE

What is Passchendaele? I have just closed a gazetteer which omits to mention it. Yet in our country it will be every schoolboy's pride to know what happened at Passchendaele. It is another Gallipoli, another Somme. Many more Australian and New Zealand troops have fought here than on Gallipoli; more than were on the Somme. Passchendaele must be mentioned along with Anzac, Lone Pine, Flers, Pozieres, Bapaume, Bullecourt and Messines …

One morning a veterinarian rode Sandy towards a ruined village. As they stopped to treat an injured mule, they heard a shell blast. Clouds of poisonous gas drifted towards them. Sandy's mask was strapped tight, but his rider's wasn't. The reins loosened and the vet fell to the ground. Sandy nudged the dying man as toxic fumes stung his own eyes.

Without a rider, Sandy galloped blindly, crashing into collapsed buildings and debris. Soldiers found him, lost and bleeding, in the barren landscape. They led him back to the veterinary hospital.

Whitfield rinsed Sandy's eyes while Archie stroked his mane and hummed. They soothed the terrified horse and dressed his wounds as best they could.

The veterinarians saved Sandy's life but they couldn't repair his eyes. Sandy's world was permanently blurry.

During three years of war, thousands of horses had died. Every Waler was needed. As soon as Sandy's scars healed he was sent back to work. Sandy had to learn to rely completely on his rider's directions.

Relentless fighting dragged on in the mud and trenches of northern France. Torrential spring rains turned the ground into a quagmire. Exhausted horses pulling heavy artillery became bogged belly-deep in mud. As Sandy helped drag them free, the horses' screams spooked him.

Each evening Archie did what he could to calm the big Waler's spirits, but Sandy's damaged eyes remained glassy with terror.

In October 1917, the Australian Defence Minister called for Major General Bridges' dying wish to be honoured. Sandy was going home at last.

'Thank goodness,' Archie cheered.

Then Archie learnt that *he* would be the groom accompanying Sandy.

'You beauty!' he yelled.

They left the Calais Veterinarian Hospital in May and their first stop was the Swaythling Remount Centre in Great Britain. Archie stayed by Sandy's side as they crossed the English Channel.

Life was peaceful in Swaythling. Sandy settled into a cosy stable with other remounts. The summer grass was sweet and Sandy heard birdsong for the first time in months.

CERTIFICATES.

Charger of the Late MAJ.GENL. W.T.BRIDGES, - G.O.C., I.T. AUST. DIVISION.

Description: Bay Gelding - Ride - 15.2 hands - 10 years - Star. Off-fore coronet white, from front-round inside to outside heel, extending up to back of fetlock - outside quarter black Ermine marks in front. Inside of off-hand coronary band white. Branded 6|D near shoulder.

CERTIFICATE "A"

Mallein Test - 14/1/18 .... NEGATIVE.

CERTIFICATE "B"

The charger in question has been in my veterinary charge since 1st.August,1915, and has been in the same camp as myself, practically ever since he arrived in Egypt in December 1914. To the best of my belief, the horse has never suffered from nor has he been in close contact with any animals suffering from DOURINE, EPIZOOTIC LYMPHANGITIS, or GLANDERS whilst in Egypt or in France.

A.P.O. 4.
B.E.F.
17/1/18.

.........................Lieut. Col.
...terinary Hospital.

"SANDY." GENERAL BRIDGE'S CHARGER.

To End His Day at Duntroon

Sandy, one of the chargers that accompanied the late General Bridges when he left Australia on the Orvieto in October, 1914, has returned to Australia. After more than four years honourable service he has been brought back — partially blind, and altogether less sleek and fiery than when he went away — to spend his remaining days in well-grassed paddocks. All the men in the First Australian Division knew Sandy, a well-bred upstanding Bay, his appearance commanded admiration, and the late General Bridges was immensely proud of him. When that splendid soldier went to Gallipoli in command of the Australian troops, Sandy remained in Egypt, and after his master's death, he found another owner. Later he was sent to France, where, after many stirring experiences he was gassed, after his rider had been killed by a fragment of shell. Sandy did not die, but the skill and care of the surgeons were powerless to save his eyesight. After many days he had recovered sufficiently to be placed on a returning transport, and arrived in Australia last week. Many thousands of horses have been sent to the war from Australia, but "Sandy" is the only one that has been returned.

In September 1918 Sandy was taken to the Liverpool docks. He pawed the wharf, reluctant to walk up *another* gangplank.

'Don't start playing up now,' Archie muttered. 'I promise this will be your last sea voyage! And before you know it, we'll be back home under that warm southern sky.'

The journey home was easier than the 1914 crossing. Sandy was the only horse on board and the weather was mild. Archie devoted all his time to grooming and exercising Sandy.

The old warhorse was never alone. Other returning soldiers fussed over him. Sandy sensed their sadness and vulnerability.

After crossing the Equator, the men's spirits lifted. Their conversations became animated as they spoke of home.

One morning, Sandy smelled eucalyptus on the sea breeze.

His cloudy eyes stared across the ocean as the scent became stronger.

Soon the men noticed it too.

'Australia,' Archie called, 'I can smell Australia!'

The *Booral* docked at Port Melbourne on 13 November 1918, two days after a peace Armistice was signed in a train carriage in northern France.

Sandy had been away for almost four years. As he clomped down the gangplank, that wobbly feeling returned.

'There now,' Archie soothed, 'you'll soon get your land legs.' But when a woman in the crowd waved, Archie's legs began trembling too.

Sandy returned to his training stable in Maribyrnong, where he grazed all day with a few paddock buddies. As 'the only one who returned' Sandy received special care and soon became legendary.

Local children came by to feed him apples. The apples were wormy but Sandy was glad to accept them. Archie visited regularly. He stroked Sandy's ears and talked about their time together in France.

Each autumn, as the leaves changed colour, a Light Horse soldier buckled Sandy's regimental saddle and led him in the Anzac Day march, honouring those who hadn't come home.

Sandy grew older.

On spring evenings, when the Bogong moths migrated, he turned north-east, holding his nose high. Sandy's nostrils quivered as he tried to catch a trace of the high-country on the breeze. He still longed for those Tallangatta hills.

Sandy was sixteen years old, frail and almost blind, when a vet came to end his suffering. Archie was there with slices of crunchy apple that smelt of alpine meadows. Sandy nickered as Archie's tears fell onto his face.

He closed his eyes. Sandy stood steady as Archie held his bridle. Whitfield joined them, then Major General Bridges marched over to rub the old Waler's ears. Sandy felt his mother's warm breath. She smelt of the high country. And there was Francis, striding across the frosty grass, whistling. Something was hidden behind Francis' back. Sandy snorted. He knew what it was. He could smell that apple.

The tired warhorse shook his mane one last time. Then he galloped away, following the wild brumbies into his beloved mountains.

Epilogue

He was one of a heroic band that worked for humanity — patiently, faithfully, silently, and then laid down toil-wracked bodies for the same cause. Far from the land of their birth they worked — and far from that land they died; all save one: Sandy.

— Sydney Evening News, 13 September 1923

A statue of Sandy, the only Australian horse to return from WWI, and Bess, from New Zealand, graces Albany's Mount Clarence, the hill that Sandy saw in October 1914. The bronze eyes of the warhorses gaze over the waters of King George Sound; that last sight of Australia for so many servicemen and women.

The Desert Mounted Corps Memorial commemorates members of the Australian Light Horse, the New Zealand Mounted Rifles, the Imperial Camel Corps and the Australian Flying Corps who lost their lives in Egypt, Palestine and Syria during WWI.

Between 1914 and 1918 Australia sent 136,000 horses overseas. In all, it's estimated that over 8 million horses died on WWI battlefields.

Six months after Sandy's death, in December 1923, Archibald Jordan also died. He was 43 years old. Some say he died of a broken heart.

Acknowledgements

Sandy's story has fascinated me since I researched *Light Horse Boy* almost fifteen years ago. Over the years I've jotted notes, but was too busy to go further. Several people sparked the next stage: the late Richard Crispin, related to the O'Donnell family who donated Sandy to Major General Bridges and the war effort, and also a member of the Tallangatta 'Sandy the War Horse Memorial Committee', a group fundraising to create a life-size sculpture of Sandy. I'd also like to thank Jean Merbach, Ross and Bryan Smith, Louise Coulston and Robyn Wood. Other high country residents, Dr Honor Auchinleck (granddaughter of General Sir Harry Chauvel) and her husband Colonel Mark Auchinleck have offered valuable insight and encouragement.

In Western Australia, I am indebted to David Theodore, curator at the Princess Royal Fortress, who has given creative and military advice since the first drafts. Thank you Justine Grey, for generously gifting me the Light Horse manual that appears in this book. It belonged to Verner Alan Emmett, who died at Gallipoli after administering first aid to a comrade. Thank you to Kathryn and John Shapland, owners of the Recollections of War Museum. Other Albany collaborators include 'The War Cabinet': Sue Buckingham, Joy Bradley and Robyn Murray, as well as Tracey Bridges, the great, great granddaughter of Major General Bridges, who by happy coincidence now lives in Albany. Tracey's family anecdotes gave flesh to Major General Bridges. Thanks also to Greta Wass from the Australian War Memorial and Stuart Smith for the Albany image. Fellow writer friends have been with me throughout the writing journey, guiding drafts of *The Last Light Horse*. A huge thank you to Deb Fitzpatrick, Kate Woodward, Maree Dawes, Barbara Temperton, Beth Kirkland, Emma Crook, Sian Turner and Venetia Marshall. Your help is greatly appreciated.

Thank you to wonderful Brian Simmonds for the stunning illustrations which light up Sandy's story. I'm so glad we could share another book journey.

Accolades to the fabulous team at Fremantle Press. Publisher, Cate Sutherland, has shepherded all four 'Light' titles to publication and I'm grateful again for her wise and creative editing. Thank you to CEO Jane Fraser, Marketing Manager Claire Miller and her team, and everyone else at this great independent publishing house. Thank you to designer Rebecca Mills for her wonderful work in bringing all the elements together so beautifully. Thank you too, to my agent, Clive Newman.

Finally, and most importantly, thank you to my family. For much of her thirty years, my daughter, Sophie, has read and edited my work. My stories are stronger for her intelligent and honest advice. Home for my sister, Karen, is a remote mountain in the Snowy Mountains with her partner Owen and their daughter Toli. Their love and appreciation for the high country infuses this book, and my mother Audrey's lifelong recitals of Banjo's famous poems helped stir my interest in bush horses. For encouraging and supporting my creative journey, thank you to my husband, Pete, and other members of our broader family.

By necessity, historical fiction leaps between factual truth and imagination; perhaps more so in this book than previous titles in the 'Light' series. Whilst Australian WWI military record keeping for humans is thorough, this is rarely the case for animals that served. Where no primary source exists, I have relied on oral history. Examples include the meeting of Major General Bridges and Sandy, believed to have occurred in the Upper Murray, but probably not at this particular saleyard muster. Little is known about the months after Sandy left Egypt and arrived at Calais. He suffered an accident where his veterinarian rider died, and his eyesight was damaged, but at the time of writing, details are not known. The major general did have two other horses, Pascha and another, referred to in a photograph as 'the brown mare'. There are many other examples where Sandy fiction meets historical truth. Please visit my website www.diannewolfer.com for more anecdotes and specific examples of these overlaps.

Photo credits: page 11 Francis O'Donnell (Sandy the War Horse Memorial Committee Incorporated); brumby and wombat (Karen Davidson); created news articles based on various reports; page 12 Horse muster (AWM P01825.005); Horses in yard (AWM 051332); page 15 Soldiers and horses galloping (AWM A03315); Light Horse Manual donated to author by Justine Grey, cover and more transcripts throughout; page 19 Three horses on ship (AWM PS0091); Major General Bridges swap card image (Kathryn and John Shapland/Recollections of War Museum); Manual; page 20-21 Calisthenics (AWM P08286.082); Draughts (AWM P08286.056); Inoculations (AWM P08286.065); Manual; page 24 Horses exercising (AWM PS0063); Departure (AWM ART00190); Ship stables (AWM P08286.015); page 28 C.E.W. Bean (AWM G01561); Unloading horses (AWM P00821.001); Horses at pyramids (AWM H02724); page 32 C.E.W. Bean on pyramid (AWM G01658); Camel (David Theodore/Princess Royal Fortress Military Museum); Stable horses (AWM J02147); page 34-35 Binoculars (AWM G00881); Gallipoli boats (AWM A02781); Digging in at Gallipoli (Alamy); page 38-39 Funeral Canberra (AWM P10797.002); Reversed boot (AWM 087280); created news articles; page 44 Procession (AWM G01494); page 48 Gas masks (AWM K00035); Burying horse (AWM E02183); created news article; page 51 Calais Veterinary Hospital (AWM E04433); Vets (AWM E04472); Horse operation (AWM E04439); page 55 Ypres ruins (AWM E00717); created news articles; Keep the Home Fires Burning lyrics/score (UK Photo and Social History Archive); page 58 Horses in mud (AWM E00963); page 60-61 Horses on Dock (AWM PB1313); Sandy's discharge papers (Richard Crispin); created news article; page 68 Sandy (AWM RELAWM00300); page 71 Albany Desert Mounted Corps Memorial (Stuart Smith); page 73 Two men and horses (AWM DAX2346).